The Adventures of Charlie

The Adventures of Charlie

ROBERT KITTLE

urlink
PRINT & MEDIA

1603 Capitol Ave., Suite 310 Cheyenne, Wyoming USA 82001
1-888-980-6523 | admin@urlinkpublishing.com

URLink Print and Media is committed to excellence in the publishing industry.

Book design copyright © 2024 by URLink Print and Media. All rights reserved.

Published in the United States of America

Library of Congress Control Number: 2024919813
ISBN 978-1-68486-917-6 (Paperback)
ISBN 978-1-68486-921-3 (Digital)

16.09.24

As the crimson sun rose slowly over the large red barn with it's rays gleaming off the gray steel roof, the animals gathered for a meeting.

"It has to go", demanded the pig with a loud snort.

"Yes, it does. It's too noisy," remarked the cow.

"Neigh, neigh" agreed the horse with such enthusiasm a loud noise rang from the pasture. A chorus of cheering rang out as one said, "Yes, we can't go around the yard without having to run for our lives".

"It's done then. It has to go!" the animals exclaimed. The animals jumped for joy. But that was shorted lived for at that moment a hen came scurrying around the corner crackled loudly. "It's coming, it's coming!"

The animals started running back to their pens as fast as their legs could carry them. Just as the last pig jumped back into the cold thick mud, the farmer, who was a tall man in his own right with long lanky legs and large feet that ate up the dirt with each stride, came across the barnyard. His new shimmering long haired black and white Border collie puppy, came around the corner. The first thing that little fur ball did was take a flying leap right into the chicken coop! Hearing the ruckus Charlie caused the farmer turned around and yell, "Hey, get out of there!" But the puppy just kept chasing the chickens around the square fenced coop, as the farmer kept on yelling.

One of the chickens said to the other, "I'll get him out!", and with that she grasped his long black bushy tail giving it a sharp yank with her sharp orange beak. The pup let out a loud yelp and ran with his tail tucked between his back legs back to the farmer. The farmer looked at the pup with amusement in his old eyes saying and said, "Well, Charlie, I told you!" He checked Charlie's tail and patted him on his black with white spotted head, then continued walking to the large red barn.

When they arrived, Charlie who was panting hard from chasing the Black and white cows, around the lush green pasture finally sat down next to an elderly Black and white Cow, named Bell. She looked down and said in a quivery voice," So~ you are the little pup that is making all the fuss"

"Yup, that's me Super Pup!"

"Oh yes", well then I guess I should say something to you", Casually remarked Bell, as she looked him over with a sinister playfulness in her eyes. He was so interested in Bell that Charlie almost got stepped on by the farmer.

"Move Charlie!" snapped the farmer with an angry voice, Charlie moved closer to Bell.

"What were you going to tell me"? As Charlie turned his attention back to the old cow.

Bell looked at him and then looked over at the other cows saying, "You know all the playing you do really irritates the animals around the barn yard. We are going to ask you to please tone it down a little."

"You mean stop"? "Replied Charlie with a shocked look in his eye, "Why"? "I am not hurting anyone or anything!"

"Yes, you are right, but you could and that would be bad for all of us and you." She watched as he tried reasoning this out, all the while hoping he would figure it out.

How" Asked Charlie tilting his head to one side?

"If you should injure one of the animals then the farmer would have to put you on a leash and you wouldn't be able to run free! (Why she thought this a good idea; she had to make him see it first?)

"In that case perhaps I shouldn't try and play with the other animals." He gave her a lopsided grin only a pup could give.

"Good!" Then looking over to the other cows she remarked," See you can talk some sense to dogs!" At that moment Charlie decided to take off after a hen and her chicks.

"CHARLIE', "CHARLIE', yelled the farmer

"CHARLIE', Yelled Bell and the others all in unison. But Charlie just kept on running, oblivious to the calls and warnings he was given.

Chapter 2

Later that night the animals gathered again for a heated meeting regarding Charlie and his behavior. "Well", squeaked the pig with frustrated,

"What you told him today did nothing at all. In fact I think it made him worse!" (At that the pig with an angry huff flopped down into his cool mud hole.)

"O.K., so that talk didn't go so well", replied Bell.

"Not at all!" yelled all of the animals.

"I'll try again, tomorrow," Bell replied with an aggregated tone

"What's the use?" Asked the horse as his tail swishing from side to side and stomped his hoof.

He's just a pup and you know as well as I, that he will not listen to us.

"Yes, I know, but we'll have to try harder that means all of us not just me" Bell said with frustration.

"How can we, when we are always running from him?" clucked the chickens.

Then a ghostly voice rang from the shadows. "Then, stop running from him and stand your ground! He is still young just play with him, teach him what he has to do. But don't let him over power you". As the animals looked for the voice, they saw Piper, the old white goat with brown spots, appeared into the light of the big yard light at the end of the big red barn.

"Piper!" shrieked Bell "Where have you been? This is the second meeting and now you show your face?"

"Yes." Said the pigs glaring at the goat "Why should we listen to you,"?

Piper's old eyes gleamed with anger in the light as he started to say, "To begin with, I am one of the elders, and another reason is I was here "with the old dog", He looked around at the group after making his statement. "You have a point but why should we listen to a goat that thinks the stall is his ramming post clucked the chickens? With a sneer on his lip and a rough tone in his voice Piper went on to say, you could at least try it and see what happens.

The horse and Bell looked at each other; then at Piper and said to the others, "We think we should take Piper's advice and see what happens." All agreed dubiously and went back to their pens. All excited to see if the new plan would work like Piper had hoped.

Chapter 3

That morning they all took Piper's advice and stood their ground. Charlie kept on with his fun and games. Not stopping to think for a minute about what he had been warned about.

"Having fun today?" Queried Bell with sarcasm dripping from every word

"No, the animals aren't fighting back, whined Charlie It isn't any fun if they are not chasing me." Why weren't they chasing me? Are they all ill? He just couldn't figure it out.

With a wicked thought Bell said, "I've an idea. Why don't you run to the other barn?"

"Why?" Charlie thought he had his hands full here, how could he possibly squeeze in anymore play mates in at this time?

"There's a goat named Piper that you should talk to", Bell said sneeringly.

Charlie looked puzzled. A goat named Piper he repeated.

"Yes" Bell replied with an evil smile."

"Maybe he would like to play!" Charlie said hopefully while his tail wagged a mile a minute and his tongue hung out the side of his mouth with the prospect of a new playmate.

"Perhaps" she sneered as she watched him race off.

Off went Charlie like a blur of fur to find Piper.

"Have fun while it lasts!" she sang to no one in particular as she dipped her head back into the feed bucket. With that she laughed. The other black and white cows looked at her. She grinned from the side of her mouth. They did not know what she had just done.

Chapter 4

Charlie raced to find Piper. In no time he found him head butting the old square oak pen in the corner of the smaller old red barn in which he lived. Butt after butt Piper hit his head on the oak rails of his pen until he heard. "Hi, what are you doing?" from a very out of breath young pup.

Piper said nothing. Again Charlie asked, "What are you doing?" Still nothing, "Bell sent me, as he tipped his head to the side, hoping with that he would get a response from the old white and brown goat. Piper drank some water out of the black tub in his pen and replied "I know why you are here he sternly replied" shaking his head vigorously

"Oh, a very excited Charlie jumped around and asked? So what are WE going to do?"

Charlie still excited was thinking what they should do first, maybe tag or hide-n-seek? But that was short lived when the goat, stomped his hoof and snorted then said firmly "WE are *not* doing anything, Charlie, just going over some rules of the yard that you must follow or there will be trouble. Sit down and let's get started, "said a very aggravated Piper. "Rules"? exclaimed Charlie tilted his head to one side like most dog do when they are totally confused

"Right, rules," Repeated Piper" What are they for "Charlie protested" never hearing of this game before, hoping to himself that it would be a fun game!

Piper cleared his throat and stared hard at the over excited pup, wondering how he was the one given this great task to give the ground rules for the barnyard to this over eager pup. First," he said pacing in his pen" never chase the livestock. Charlie's head dropped "thinking to himself, what fun is that. "This game is not fun at all so far". "Second," piper exclaimed always do what the farmer says." "But" Charlie start to say as Piper cut him off, The most important rule of all, Piper's eyes got very big and an uneasiness fell over Charlie like he wanted to run but couldn't. He was trapped in Piper's gaze, Piper's hair on his back stood up, then slowly but with force stated. ...DON'T DO ANYTHING BELL SAYS!"

Charlie was very confused at the last rule. "I thought Bell was my friend though?" inquired Charlie, with a confused look on his face.

"You thought wrong", as the old goat put his hoof on the railings he was hitting to get a better look at Charlie, and to make sure he could hear what he had just said to him.

"She is not as nice as she appears, Watch out" Now if you don't mind, please leave my part of the barn, but remember what I told you about the rules? Most of all remember the one about Bell," Piper's "old face went blank "as he said this to Charlie. I really don't want you to get hurt by her. You have a lot of growing up to do but I know you will be just fine if you keep your distance from that old Black and white Cow." Pipe started to "snicker a little" and with a gleem in his eye looked at Charlie and laughed. Now we are going to put on a bit of a show for the sake of the rest of the livestock, I will chase you out of my barn"

"OK?" questioned Piper to Charlie.

"I'm game!" Replied a bouncing Charlie like he was a spring toy. With a wink from the old goat's eye, he chased Charlie out of the barn and back to the nice green grass around the little white house were the farmer lived. Hoping that the Little Pup would keep in mind everything he had just told him.

Chapter 5

Later that day in the green meadow behind the big red barn, Bell had an idea for a little trip to have Charlie go visit a friend at another farm down the street. She thought it was so great she had to tell the other cows."

"Do you think he'd get hurt or killed?" Asked the others. They certainly didn't like Charlie chasing them all the time, but they were a hundred percent sure that they didn't want to see him get hurt badly. However a little lesson would be fine to teach him they supposed.

"If he does it will take care of the problem" snapped Bell with a smile that would make any animal run and hide until it was safe.

"But we think the problem is taking care of itself with Piper's idea." They still had reservations about the whole thing, but who were they to interfere with Bell "being the meanest cow on the farm and all"!

"Yes the problem is resolved but I'd like to have a little fun," Bell was saying as she ambled away from the others. She called out for the black and white puppy dog. "Charlie, oh Charlie, where are you? I must talk to you. I have something for you to do for me if you could please!" The little pup came scooting around the corner of the barn at full speed, almost taking out a group of chickens feeding on some corn on the ground. "I am here I am here," Charlie yelled, as he came speeding up to her, ever ready to help and forgetting everything that Piper had told him.

"I hate to do this but could you be a dear and", Bell stopped and put her head down like she was upset over something, then said.

"You see we can't get out of here so you must go the Harvey's Farm for us. It is across the meadow". It's a much larger farm than ours, with four big white barns, gray roofs, and a house that looks like something out of the movie."

Why do I have to do this for you?", questioned a very confused but excited Charlie? "Because I can't get over the fence. Only you can give the message." Bell said carefully. "Your message will be to tell the bull that he is not the strongest animal on the block anymore! Tell him that you are. Then prove it." Charlie flipped his head up and looked at Bell. He then responded to her with a question in his voice. "Piper told me not to do anything you say."

"Oh he did, did he?" Bell retorted with a fire in her eyes, at the unpleasant news.

Charlie, not realizing he had set the ball rolling continued on. "He also said that you may want to hurt me in some way!"

"Now why would I want to do that?" Looking down at her hoofs which were hiding in the tall grass. "You do what you think is right "BUT" With a sound of nerves and a smile that dripped with questionable ethics "I hear there is dog bone in it for you and not one of those small one."

As soon as Charlie heard that he went screaming off to the other Farm like a F16 jetfighter to a battle zone, as well as muttering something about that bull. The other cows watched as Charlie flew off. As they were a safe distance from Bell they expressed, "This can't be good, what shall we do?" They looked at each other and uttered "what will we do, if we stop him then we have to deal with…" they stopped as Bell ambled past the group with her head high and an evil smile still on her face. "Ladies" she pronounces as she walked past the group. They looked at each other with a look like "yea good point we don't want to have to deal with that". They just watch the pup fly to the other farm praying that nothing will happens to him.

Chapter 6

When Charlie arrived at the farm he was very tired from running so he took a nap. He slept under a large oak tree overlooking the corn fields and the lake in the meadow. As he slept he had a dream. He was home chasing the chickens around the barns with the other small animals. The farmer was shouting at him so he stopped and looked at him. While he was asleep, the cows in the field started to gather around him. And one started nudging him. Then Charlie woke up come to find it was not the cows nudging him but a very large black with a white strip down its head and white hoofed bull!

"Who are you?" Inquired the very large, very mean bull

"I'm Charlie, he snarled I live at the neighbor's farm". He scrambled to his feet

"Why are you here?"Demanded the bull who was ten times the size of the pup.

"Because, Bell told me to tell you that there was a stronger animal in town and that is me!" he proudly announced like he was instructed to do.

The bull laughed, "Well I guess we'll have to see." With that remark he charged Charlie. Who at that moment was not so sure he should be there anymore? With that he ran but the bull being the size he was, over powered him before he could get away. He flipped him across the meadow, as Charlie laid there he thought of what Piper had said about Bell and hurting him. Now he did not know what was going to happen to him. Then things started to go dark.

Meanwhile across the field, the farmer was looking for Charlie, "Here Charlie, here boy! Where is that fur ball?" The farmer rambled all over the yard, barns, chicken coops, and the meadows. There was no sign of him any where. The farmer was getting worried and muttered. "I'll give him an hour then I will take a drive. Maybe he went down the road." He ambled back to the house. By now old Bell was splitting her sides laughing at the farmer running around trying to find his friend.

"What's so funny?" declared the others.

"The farmer can't find his dog right?" she laughed cruelly

"Right" they didn't like this one bit. Something didn't feel right. There was something wrong here very wrong

"I sent him down the road to go after the bull". By this time if she had been drinking milk it would be coming out her nose as hard as she was laughing. "I can only guess what shape he is in, if any". The entire barnyard went silent like a switch had turned off. Bell looked around and shouted with a force, "Well, you said you wanted him gone and I did just that and I don't feel a bit bad about it!"

"I told that pup not to listen to you!" barked an old cold voice from the barn. All of the others knew the voice. It was Piper and he was extremely irritated.

"Well he did and there is nothing you can do about it" By now Bell and Piper were standing head to head.

You sent the little pup to an early grave and for what? Because none of you could take care of yourselves, is that it? "Piper was steamed. If it was not for the fact there were others around he would have had a heart to heart with Bell. There was muttering amongst the animals. Then Piper continued, "Let's just hope he comes back in one piece. If he doesn't, let's all remember who put him there glaring in Bell's direction. He marched back to his pen to let off some steam the best way he knew how by butting his head against his oak pen.

Chapter 7

With all the events in the few minutes, there was not a lot of action going on . Everyone pretty much kept to themselves the rest of the day. Later on that evening when the sun was turning a fiery shade of orange, setting over the small pond with the willow tree in the corner, the phone rang in the little white house where the farmer lived. "Hello" said the farmer with a sound of fright' in his voice, "yes I am looking for him. No, I haven't found him." There was a pause, then the farmer like some one just hit him with a pitch fork in his foot, yelled he's where? He did what? How did he? Why did he? The farmer was falling over his words as if he was falling down a hill. I will be right there. The farmer threw down the phone and ran out the door, like he had just received a call that he won a million dollars and had to get it right then. He jumped in his truck and sped off like he was in a NASCAR race. Some of the animals that heard the phone ring and saw the farmer were looking at each other , "What do you think is going on?" utter a hen from the group standing around where the farmers truck was sitting a minute ago.

"It had to be about Charlie. Why else would he run out like that and yell as he did when on the phone, replied the pig from its pen adjacent to the truck's parking spot. "Maybe the bull did get the little guy. What a shame if he did. "Maybe", said Bell, "Maybe." She walked by all the others who by this time were looking at her in a different light. She waddled out to the other end of the meadow. She wanted to eat in peace. All the time thinking to herself what a great job she did removing the little fur ball from her farm.

Bell was in the meadow by herself by the time Piper ambled over to the group. They was still standing where the farmer's truck busted out of there not moments ago. The horse with his golden hair and brown mane as tall as a full grown man, looked down at Piper with a bit of concern in his voice asked. "I am going to guess from all the commotion that has just happened in the last few minutes, from you yelling at Bell and the farmer yelling on the phone, I missed something"? the horse retorted, "I know you talked to Charlie, Piper, but I don't know what it was. So could someone please clue me on to what is going on", as he reared up in agitation,

"OK calm down don't get all worked up. I will tell you" Piper declared. He went on by saying "I told him in short not to chase us and not to do anything Bell says." Then the other animals which were around for the phone call that the farmer received, filled in the horse on the rest.

By now the horse was madder than a cat being pushed into a bucket of water. He stumped his hoofs and looked out to where Bell was still eating. The horse stopped staring at Bell then looked at Piper and the others and shouted out "Bell has always caused trouble like this, but I think this maybe the worst thing she has ever done. Why in the world would she have told him to go over there in the first place? And what the heck did he get into for the farmer to fly out of here like that". The horse still irritated paused for a bit. Then Piper busted out with "I don't know but I sure would like to find out."

There was a lull in the crowd that had gathered after the horse's outrage. Then a small voice came from the back. "I know" said the voice "I know what Bell told the Charlie. I will tell you the rest if you promise not to tell Bell." Then out of the back of the crowd came a very small but pretty cow with white all over but on her head and back were two black spots. By now she was in the front and all of them were looking at her. Piper strolled over to the little cow and said in a sweet voice that no one knew he had, "It's ok child you can tell us, what she said to the pup for him to do whatever he did." She then related what Bell told Charlie and what he would get if he did it. She also told them that Charlie did bring up what Piper had said to him which Bell was not pleased to hear that. But he must of thought the prize must have been too great to overlook the danger. By the time she was done Piper was as mad as a goat could be like being in a cramped pen for about a week.

"I can't believe she would do that. How mean can she be?" Piper thought he had seen everything from that cow but this one topped the cake. She didn't just remove the problem, she may have just killed it off. Piper looked at everyone in the group and pronounced "if she would do that to him what else does she have going on in that head of hers?". Piper looked around and the Pig which was now looking through the horse legs to see what the heck was going on said, "I don't know but let's keep the conversation low." With a nudge of his head Piper looked over to find Bell strolling over to the group, like nothing had ever happen and must be talking about the weather.

"Did I miss the meeting?" Innocently remarked Bell when she made it to the middle of the crowd.

"No, there wasn't a meeting!" they said. "We were just talking."

"All good I hope"? Asked Bell "Was it about how I got rid of the dog problem?" She asked as if she should have a band playing something like "hail to the chief."

"Why yes! Yes it was," snarled Piper, with a look of something being plotted in his mind.

"I know I am so good you can kiss my hoofs now if you wish". She winked "I must leave and go with the other cows it is almost milking time. We must not be late for that." She put her head in the air and flounced away to the big red barn where the cows were heading to get milked. Piper looked at her strutting away and uttered under his breath, "Go get milked". The other cows gasped saying "that wasn't nice", true however it is where she is going, but how you said it was not nice". The other cows were soon heading down there as well. Piper and the others went back to their barns. They all were waiting to see how things would work out for the pup.

What seemed like days the animals finally heard the farmers' truck motoring up the drive. It had an eerie sound to it like it was moving at a very slow pace much slower than they have heard before. He stopped close to the house and opened the door slowly and said, "We are home give me a sec and I will get you in the house". The farmer stepped out of the truck and shut the door. He walked around to the front of the truck to open the other door. The animals which had come out of their hiding places for a closer look to see what would come out. Most were hoping it was Charlie and he would just jump out of the truck, and be ready to go. But when the door opened there was no ball of fur running out jumping on the grass, looking for something to chase but a just a pup almost lifeless laying on the seat.

"Let me through said a forceful voice let me through". Bell pushed her way through the crowd to see what there was to see. She saw that the farmer had Charlie in the truck patched up and not in a box.

"Well" she uttered with emotion putting her head in the air as if there was a smell she didn't like, "I guess I didn't do a good enough job after all, he's still here". The farmer scooped Charlie up from the front seat of the truck. But there was little to no movement coming from the pup.

Someone in the crowd said with teary voice "He looks dead". There was a cold silence over the group after that was said.

"I hope you are happy", retroted a very angry goat. "If I was just a little taller I would ram you right in the!"... as he stopped himself before he tried to do it anyway.

"But, you are not, so you can't!" declared Bell, with a self important arrogance to her tone and a smirk that any good mother would like to remove of her face. The farmer walked by with the dog still limp. Charlie opened his eyes just enough to see and said in a very weak voice so low you could almost not hear him. "Sorry, Bell, I tried. He got me before I could finish playing. I don't think he liked what I told him very much Bell I don't know." Then he shut his eyes again.

"That's OK" Bell shouted with a tone that was far from mother like. "When you get stronger we'll have a go at it again". Bell and the others watched as the farmer walked in his front door of his little white house and let out of deep breath. As the group was breaking up the voice that every one knew so well, and would love not to hear again for a long time spoke out,

"Well he'll never bother us again!" Bell remarked with a grin. She turned to head back to the barn for the night but was stopped by a group of animals that she thought would be on her side. Right in her way and a little taller was the horse who had made his stance on the ground and was not moving from that spot. Then encircling Bell was no other then her sister cows. In the middle of this circle right in front of the horse was none other than Piper. His horns pointed at her and his front hoof pawing the ground.

"Let me through!" demanded Bell, "Why are you doing this" What is your problem? I want to go back to the barn". Bell tried to get around them but no matter how hard she tried they just surrounded her with Piper still acting like he was going to attack.

After a few minutes and Bell still trying to get away, Piper lifted his head slowly and with authority. His eyes looked as though fire would shoot out of them. Then he proclaimed. "For starters" snorted Piper, "What in the world were you thinking, I am guessing you weren't" Piper stopped looked around as if he was looking for right words to say. Then he continued "If that was your calf would you let him play with a wolf?" Bell by now glaring at Piper and still not letting her pass lifted her one eye brow and shout at him,

"NO, are you crazy who would be that stupid! The calf would be eaten by the wolf."

Piper snapped right back with

"What do you think about the farmer?" That DOG is like his child, and he could have been one of our friends". Piper turned from them but had this to say, "We will let you go but keep in mind that maybe just maybe someday that dog might save your life."

"No dog is going to do anything for me! Can you believe this ram? I think you have hit that pen too many times. Come on girls let's go to the barn and eat". As she turned to look back she saw that no one was going to follow her. They were all still standing there looking at her like she had just turned green with blue spots. Bell by now very upset with her so called friends uttered, "Fine I will go and eat alone! I don't need you gals!" as she stormed off to the barn, talking under her breath.

After she was out of view the others turned to Piper and asked with great worry, "What should we do?" Piper, looked down at the ground then replied

"For right now we'll hang low and see what happens in a few days or so". He then continued with a plan, "This is what we will do. Chickens you go to the house and find the dog to see how he is". The chickens looked at Piper and asked "will he chase us"? Piper stopped and replied "I don't believe he will chase you", with a smile he announced "In fact I know he won't because he is too weak. Next I will amble over and see if I can talk to him". After saying that an evil laugh came out of the goat. He looked around and in a low voice and said "Then we will fix Bell".

"Fine", said the chickens we will do it. They felt like at least it wasn't too late to fix this terrible wrong that they helped make.

Chapter 8

For the longest time Charlie was nowhere to be seen. They knew he was in the house for the farmer sounded like he was talking to him. But the animals couldn't see him because they couldn't get close enough to the house to look in the windows. Then after what felt like a year on a nice warm morning after the dew was off the grass and the sun made the shadows of the trees seem to disappear, one of the chickens that was on watch for the pup came scurrying to the barn moving it's feet so fast there was nothing but a orange blur. The horse which at this time was chilling in the shade of the old barn shouts out across the barn yard, "Piper get over here! The chicken is coming"! Piper ran out of his barn like a pack of wolves was after him. By that time he was where the horse was as the chicken was just skidding to a stop.

The chick's breath finally caught up with her, and in as loud of a voice she could muster she said, "He's out he's out". She was dancing around the two animals as if the soldier was coming home from war. The Chicken continued by saying, "With the help of the farmer by putting Charlie on the porch with a pillow to lay on".

"Well" Piper said with a gleam in his eye and a smile, "I guess now would be a good time to go see how things are going" Piper headed towards the House to see Charlie.

Charlie was laying on the pillow looking over the field of rolling green grass, and thinking how close he came to not seeing any of this again. He was interrupted by a old voice that Charlie knew well saying.

"Sure is a nice day, how are you doing sport?" Questions Piper as he ambled onto the porch where Charlie was laying and sat next to him.

Charlie slowly lifted his head and looked right into Pipers eyes. Piper could tell that he was still in a lot of pain, but was still glad to have him there. Charlie opened his mouth and in a low still in a painful voice replied "I've been better". He then looked back over the meadow of green grass and watched as the wind danced across the grass tops, like a top spinning around on a dance floor, Charlie without even looking over to see if the goat was still there retorted, "You know what Piper?" Piper not knowing what was on the pup's mind hesitated a little before saying,

"What?" Charlie with the look of hurt and pain in his eyes looked back at the old goat. Then said, I should have listened to you. He whimpers as he moved to get a better look at the goat. Piper could see the stitches wrapped with bandages. The pain the dog was still in was almost too much for him to bear. He calmly said in a kind voice," Charlie "we all have to learn at some point, just like Bell will need to learn the wrong she has done". Charlie with the best puzzled look he could give at the time, looked right at Piper and with a short gasp of air said.

"But I thought Bell is my friend!" There were tears starting to form in the young dogs eyes, as if someone just took his favorite toy away. Piper seeing this glared right at him eye to eye and snorted "Oh, is she?" The sarcasm rolled off his tongue like ice cream from a cone.

"Yes, I thought" Retorted a very hurt and confused Charlie.

Piper still glaring at the dog confused at what was going on, continued with "Would a friend have you go to different farm. A farm mind you that you are not supposed to go to in the first place? Then on top of it all you pick on a bull, a very mean bull at that? Do you think a good friend would do that to you WELL"? Piper said it with such force that Charlie was getting scared of him sitting next to him. It was so bad that Charlie tried to move over but couldn't since he was in too much pain still, Charlie still thinking if he should try to move somehow even if that meant being in more pain. Just gave in and proclaimed with as much voice as he had," you don't think much of Bell do you. Then again" he continued "I never thought of that!" Charlie then thought back to what Bell has asked him, to do. Was it really that improtant to do in the first place? Piper finally finished his preaching to Charlie. He looked Charlie over very good. With a flip of his tail and a twist in his neck proclaimed "You got lucky this time, but next time it may not be the case." Charlie rolled his eyes like someone had already said that once. Out of side of his mouth said "yes that's what the vet said." He then tried to move but let out a loud yelp. this scared a bird in the tree that overlooked the corner of the house and the porch. Where at this moment was his home.

"You still have a lot of problems don't you"? replied the goat still looking him over "You have, I see three broken legs, which means you only have one good one to stand on". The goat sneered which was trying to cover up a laugh. He just made a joke that he thought was pretty good.

Charlie then added to his problems by saying he also had three broken ribs. They almost put him down, but the farmer saved him from that. Piper sat with the pup most of that afternoon until the shadows on the trees grew longer and the sun was getting orange and lower in the sky. "Well I must start back to the barn now and the farmer will be taking you in soon". Piper then got up and walked off the porch and down to the barn where he called home. Then he stopped and looked like he was thinking. Then turned around and asked."When will you be able to run" with a little bit of a question building in his voice. "Not for a month or so" replied Charlie once again he gave the one eye brow look to his old friend ." Ok then that will give us a lot of time to plan Bell's surprise". He snorted and strolled of leaving Charlie on the porch more confused then before. Charlie then yelled to his friend "what surprise"? Piper just turn and said, "We will talk more tomorrow. Good night". He then went into his barn as the farmer walked out the door picked up the pup and replied, "ok buddy time to come in for the night. You can come back out tomorrow if it is nice", With that he walked back in and shut the white door on his little white house.

Chapter 9

Now with all he had done to himself with broken legs and the ribs the next few weeks were tough for Charlie. He couldn't do anything for himself. If he had to go in or out, the farmer moved him around but for the most part he pretty much stayed outside on his pillow looking over the meadow watching the other animals running around wishing he was out there to. Sure the chickens and the horse would come to the fence to talk to him. Piper would come over most days, but it just wasn't the same sitting day after day.

"Well I am glad you're all right", the horse replied with a long face like he wish he could have done something before this happened. "What Bell did was an inexcusable thing to do.

"Yes, I have been told this many times already, and I should have listen to Piper", sighed Charlie in a heavy voice, while rolling his eyes up in his head hoping that Piper would be coming up to hear any part of that. "But" he continued with a very straight face, "None of you would have cared if I had died," with a hint of sorrow in his small voice. He didn't blame them one bit if that was how they felt. After all, he did make their lives rough chasing them all the time.

"Not all of us, pup," an elderly voice was heard. Piper was slowly ambling up from the barn. "Not all of us dislike you. I for one think you are an alright pup. You just need some fine tuning."

Charlie's ears flipped up when he heard that. His tail was now starting to swing back and forth like it was trying to swipe the porch. For the first time in weeks he felt that someone liked him" Do you think you" he stopped and looked around and then said "all of you could help me?" the animals looked at each other, then at Charlie, then at Piper who was looking at each one them. They all really did care about Charlie, as he looked at each one. With that tail moving and those eyes those big black eyes with so much love and hope in them how could they say yes.

After a few minutes all were looking around hoping someone would say something. A bright white chicken with a red comb walked up to Charlie and looked into his black eyes and asked "Would it be a problem for you to stop chasing us around the yard. It is getting old very quick having to look over our backs all the time?"

"YES" exclaimed the group and stop chasing all of us though the mud! Then the chicken thought, and with her eyes looking up to the blue sky "What will the pigs do?" Then over Charlie's shoulder he heard a pig grunt at the chicken and the sound of the mud splashing around.

"Also" the white chicken went on to say "the calves and the colts, getting them worked up is not a good thing to do either. Wouldn't you agree"? The chickens looked over to the cows and the horse which were just on the other side of the fence next to the house under a great apple tree. They both at the same time looked at Charlie and closed their eyes and shook their heads. Then the chicken looked back at Charlie.

He looked around at the group that was now around him. He put his head on his paws and with a little sadness in his voice said, "Yes, I will." A chorus of cheers rang through the barnyard as one by one they stated that they would be more than happy to help him. Piper looked at them and at Charlie then with a smile and eyes fixed on the barn where Bell was most of the time moved his head slowly back to Charlie and uttered , "We will start tomorrow and no one is to talk to Bell about any of this, is that clear"! He looked around with an evil eye. Looked then at Charlie. They all agreed and went back to their pens. Piper, on the other hand stayed with Charlie, "so" Piper with his rough voice "Now that you told them you would leave them alone can you do that"? Charlie still looking down said with a smile," I guess I will have to." Then they just sat there until the sun went down with the frogs croaking and the stars shining like glitter in the sky.

Chapter 10

The next morning while the chickens were still in their coop. The sun was just shedding its light over the horizon in the corner of the meadow where the fence row turns and runs down to the barns, Bell was chewing her cud all alone. Now on a normal day the cows were all out there trying to get a bite to eat before it was time for milking. But for some reason on this day it was just her. "Where are all my friends"? She wondered as she was looked around for them waiting to see if there were in a different spot. "They are not out yet. I wonder if I missed something, or if their milking was early"? She trotted back to the barn. When she walked back through the door she saw them, just standing there. No farmer, no helper so she asked them with a weird look on her face, "You didn't come out to eat, what have you been doing in here?

"Nothing" Chorused the cows to Bell, sounding a little too nervous. When she went out to eat that morning, the cows staying back to talk about what Charlie had agreed, to and what Piper had said. They were scared that she would somehow find out and possibly take it out on them.

Bell now thinking there is something up. Then with a arrowed brow asked like it was heavy on her mind and troubling her asked with her head down "what is going on with that little pup?" Then she picked up her head so she could look at all of them. "Hmmmm," she had a smile. The other cows look at each other like she had just put on a Tutu and was dancing around the barn. They replied,

"We don't know."

Bell not convinced turned to utter "I must be off. If you'd like you can eat with me near the pond. The grass tastes much better." They once again looked at each other then replied,

"No thanks, maybe later. Mmmmm, we are not hungry right now." She turned and walked out the door swinging her tail side to side. They all let out a sigh of relief as they watched her walk away

"Wow that was close. Do you think she believed it"? asked one of the black cows with a white spot on her back right leg.

"Yes I believe she did" remarked another.

"I hope so I really don't want to do this lying thing for very long. It's not like me to do this". They walked out of the barn and into the meadow where Bell was to start eating before milking time. Unfortunately what they didn't realize was there were little ears listening. Those little ears were running to where Bell was busy eating grass by herself still trying to finger out what up with everyone. She did not see this thing coming towards her. This little animal which was now right in front of her nose shouted as loud as it could "Bell", "Bell" cried a wee little voice.

She stopped and looked around with a confused look on her face. "Is someone calling my name?" she looked around, and whispered "hello".

"Down here", replied the little voice.

She put her head down to the grass line and once again replied softly, "hello". Is that you grass, talking to me? If so I need to find a different place than the pond to eat".

"NO" yelled the little voice "I am right here" A little animal jumped up out of the tall grass on to her nose. Bell jump and screamed, like she had just found a wasps nest or something. The small animal fell to the ground with a thump. "Ouch" it cried as it turned around to face the cow which had just launched it like a water balloon. Bell once again moved her head slowly back to the ground to look at this little critter in the grass. Sitting in front of her was a little brown with big feet and along black tail field mouse. Bell, not being to fond of them, moved back a few steps. With a stern voice and a heavy brow asked. "What do you want and how do you know my name?"

"Well," the little mouse started out "that is a deep subject. Do we have time for this I have things to do. "How do you know my name", a very irritated Bell demanded. She figured since she already had been attacked from this thing and was still looking around to see if anyone saw her, dancing around like a dancer with two left feet, she had the right to know. "Finding out your name is a funny story but we don't have time for the story. Let's say we just get down to business." The mouse motioned for her to come closer, so against her better judgment she did. What is it? "she asked with her teeth clinched. "You want to know about the dog right? Then Bell moved her head to the right "You could say that," she said. The mouse continued also I would love some of that delicious grain the farmer so generously gives you at milking time. When it hits the floor I can't get there fast enough to grab it. That grain is so good and it melts in your mouth." As he was saying that his little mouth was salivating and was grossing out Bell. "So" said the mouse with a grand bit of excitement "Is it a deal"?

"It's a deal", retorted Bell. It seemed like a silly request to her, but if it gave her information, then so be it.

"Well then Mouse", Bell looked right at it. What can you tell me about why everyone is acting the way they are lately". The mouse told Bell what the cows said,

"That afternoon they were having a meeting I overheard the chickens talking about it on my way to you". The Mouse blurted out before taking a breath.

Bell now very anger at them all looked around and sarcastically remarked," Oh are they now?" Bell looked around this time making sure not a soul was around but she and the mouse and then replied. "Then I guess we will have to be there. We meaning you mouse. By the way" Bell looked at the little mouse and said "what is your name? I can't just call you mouse all the time".

At that moment the mouse stood on it back legs and made itself as tall as it could. In the biggest voice he could muster yelled out "Mack, is my name" with a grin that could light up the sky.

"Well, Mack" Bell said with a smile "You and I are going to have fun with this". She then went on to tell him that every time he gave her information on the dog and what is going on, she would give him some grain. Mack was so excited about his new business venture he had never been this brave before. Most of the time he would stay in the shadows and let others take what he wanted. But not this time! No sir this was his and no one else's. Bell Looked down at Mack after telling him the plan and asked very nicely "is that a deal then"?

"Yes," said Mack "It's a deal". He then turned and almost fell into the pond while high tailing it back to the barn to his hiding place before the farmer got in there to milk the cows. The whole time thinking how wonderful it will be to get some grain fresh out of the bag and it not falling on the ground and getting stepped on first. When the little mouse was out of sight, Bell went back to eating some grass and all the time thinking to herself. "So they have something planned for me do they? We'll see about that," with that she laughed a very evil laugh. It echoed over the meadow making the birds go silent in the trees and the frogs stop their song. She then headed up to the barn for it was time for milking.

Chapter 11

When the sun rose for a new day to start, the door opened with a creak. The farmer stepped out on to the porch carrying Charlie in his arms. "Here you are Charlie my boy", the farmer retorted with a laugh "service with a smile." He patted him on the head after laying him on the mat. The farmer then strolled down to the barn to do some work. When the farmer was out of sight all the animals gathered around Charlie, which by now had time to adjust himself to sitting better so he could see every one. There was one thing about this meeting. This time Bell had ears for at this time a little mouse name Mack, had made his way up the house door and had snuck under a broken piece of siding. This way he wouldn't be seen listening in on the meeting.

When the last chicken had hit the railing and the last pig made it out of the mud, Piper stood up and looked at his fellow animals and said, "We all know why were are here," he announced walking back and forth on the porch like a minister on Sunday Morning, "YES"! shouted the group like the voice of an army patrol heading to battle. Piper got low and started out again "this little pup was almost removed from us; it was an act that over step the boundaries of teaching a lesson, it was just plain mean." The group was getting in to the sermon that Piper was preaching. "There should be some sort of action taken, even if some of you are to blame for this pup's misfortune". The crowd hushed like a zipper had closed their mouths. They knew the goat was right. If they had listened to him from the start and stood up to Bell, then none of this would had ever happened. Piper then looked at them one by one.

"We have a choice to do something or do nothing. To do nothing would be letting her know that what she did was ok, which we can see was not. As Piper pointed his head to the pup lying on his mat next to him," SO!" Piper yelled out "The question I need to ask now will be"...

He stopped, with his lungs full of air, as he looked around again. He let out a snort out of his nose, lifted his right eye brow and said really quickly "what are we going to do'?

With that, the meeting went into full swing. Still none of them saw Mack perched on top of the door taking down notes, like the little spy he was.

"I think we should taint her food with something smelly so she will not eat it. Then her milk productions will go down and the farmer may get rid of her."

"That's a good idea if it wasn't for the fact that we eat out of the same trough", said the cows.

"O.K. we will not do that then. "Any other ideas?" asked Piper moving for corner to corner looking at each animal.

Then out of the blue and a very low voice came from the lower part of the fence.

"Well ummm." Said the voices in a serious tone.

"We could have her fall into our mud hole." All the animals stopped and looked over to the fence. Where a little pig was gleaming. like a cat that just ate the family bird.

Charlie started to laugh; "Now that would be nice to see. Just the thought of her rolling around in the mud trying to get out, would be wonderful to watch".

"Now the big question would be is how to get her to the mud hole, let alone get her to fall into it," said Piper. The groups were all thinking, the goat was pacing, while the other talked amongst themselves. Then like a light bulb that came on in the night, Charile popped his head up off the mat like a bee string him and replied,

"We could tell her I would like to talk to her, then that would get her into the pen. But that is all I have, though".

"Yes, that would work!" neighed the horse. "She would have to go into the pigpen to talk to you since my pen is closed for the moment so the colts won't get stepped on."

"Good, we will try to do it tomorrow!" Remarked Piper.

At that moment Mack found the opportunity to remove himself from the meeting and not be seen. He slide down the door, around the porch then made a bee line down the hill, between the big red barn and the smaller red barn, that piper called home and down to the field. Bell was waiting beneath a large apple tree, next to the pond where she was sitting should come after next to the pond.

"Well", what did they said?' asked Bell.

Mack read her his notes from the meeting. When he had finished Bell said," I never have seen so much fuss over a little dog in my life. The old dog and I were great friends. We would sit under this tree and talk for hours".

"I hate to stop this trip down memory lane but", Said Mack.

"Very well", said Bell bitterly." Here "she said as she threw some grain on the ground. As Mack was eating he continued, "I am glad they didn't go with the first idea.

"This grain is good", remarked the mouse as he went back to the barn.

Bell sat under the tree for a while and thought about how the animals were getting back at her and how she might get back at them. This is something she would have to think about. She got up and headed to the barn for milking time with the others whom she thought were her friends.

Chapter 12

Later that day Bell moved from the field into the barnyard to where the others were. She watched their expressions as she sauntered into their space.

"We have news for you, Bell" said the others.

"What news?" Asked Bell (In a non suspicious tone)

"Charlie would like to talk to you." (they simply remarked)

"We don't know why but the chickens came over to tell us to tell you."

"What time am I suppose to see him?"

The cows looked at each other then replied," He comes out at noon. So we guess that's when you could go over there. He sits on the back porch."

"OK I will go over tomorrow and talk to Charlie." With that she walked into her stall and put her head into the trough. She got some for Mack and smiled out of the corner of her mouth.

The next day, she was out with Mack under the apple tree, when they heard the farmer.

"Charlie, it's time to go out. Here you go on your blanket."

"Guess I'm off," said a very anxious Bell. As she was leaving Mack laughed and said, "Don't" fall in the Mud." "Don't fall in the mud."

Bell made her way to Charlie. She naturally went to the horse's pen but the horse was ready for her. "Hello Bell," he said

"Hello", I have to talk to Charlie today. I would like to take a short cut through your pen"

"The pen is closed off for the day as the little ones are in training for jumping and barrel racing",.

"Really? smirked Bell looking at the ground to keep the smile from showing. I guess I will have to use the pig pen and try not to fall in the mud hole".

"Guess so", replied the horse.

Bell headed over to the pigs' side of the farm.

"Hello", how are you?" asked the pigs.

"Hello", fine said Bell . May I please come in and talk to Charlie?"

"Why yes"

"Thanks, she said as she walked into the pen and stood next to the mud hole. She was looking, with displeasure, at the mud hole and said to the pigs. "And you lay in this?"

"We do because we do not have a pond in our pen like you do. Be careful!"

"Why?" asked Bell.

"Sometimes the piglets escape and run around the hole. Anyone near them trips and falls into the mud."

"I'll watch it", said Bell

"Just a warning and the pigs turned and walked back.

Bell looked over the fence at a taped up Charlie who was lying on his blanket. "See you're doing well".

"Just fine, if you think being taped up and resting on a blanket for an unknown amount of time is well." Said Charlie.

"I hope you can come out to the barn and talk to me soon." Said Bell

"I hope so!", said Charlie wagging his tail as if he were happy about the idea.

"We could talk about how you can go back to the bull and show him who is boss!"

"Maybe." (he thought carefully before replying next) "Does that bull ever get into your field?"

"No!"

"Then why did you send me over there, if he's never been here?"

"Well… um…well" replied Bell stammering for words. That was the sign for the piglets to come. They came around the mud hole and under Bell. But she was ready for them. She just jumped over and replied, "Just because and that's why I sent you". And ran out of the pen.

"Well, that didn't work". Said the pig. "Maybe there was too much warning".

"Or, I didn't have her think hard enough", said Charlie. "We'll talk to Piper when he gets here. Right now I have to take a nap on my blanket". With that Charlie put his head down and went to sleep. Bell jounced back to the apple tree and sat down.

Chapter 13

"How did it go", said a small voice.

"Not as well as they'd hoped", said Bell, gleefully "Guess they will be having another meeting later, I am going to see what is up." said Mack.

"Good, go see what the next plan is and there will be more grain in it for you", said Bell. Then she just laid under the tree, with the wind rustling the leaves above her. After a few minutes she finally got up and went down to the pond where she ran into Piper. "Hello, what brings you down here?" asked Bell.

"Just a drink of real water. The water in my stall is getting old like me" replied Piper

"Oh", and then Bell started to drink.

"Who were you talking to up there"? asked Piper.

Bell spit her water halfway across the pond. "Who me?" He voice quavered.

"Just heard voices and thought one was yours" replied Piper.

"I was talking to myself "

"O.K" but you know what they say about people talking to themselves"

"Yes, I do", snapped Bell. Piper walked back to his pen.

"I hope he didn't hear all the conversation. I guess Mack and I will have to change where we want to meet." That evening after milking, Bell was worried sick about Piper knowing about her spy. All night she was afraid he knew. In the morning she found Mack eating some of the grain she had given him. "We need to talk", said Bell

"Alright" replied Mack. As they walked out to the other side of the field Mack asked,

"What's up?"

"That goat heard us talking yesterday"

"Oh, that's bad!", said Mack with a look of concern afraid he wouldn't get anymore grain.

"Yes, it is. This is what we are going to do. When you go to the meeting, get there before the rest of them and go under the porch. Sit so when the meeting is finished you can escape without being seen. Then go to the third fence post left of the pond. There we can meet and talk without being overheard."

"Great", said Mack.

Chapter 14

The next meeting was that afternoon. Mack slipped under the porch. Piper was already there with Charlie. The other animals were just getting there.

"I can't believe that it didn't work", said the pig.

"Nor do I, said the horse. We had things all worked out, I thought. What do you think went wrong?"

Piper thought and said, "The element of surprise was not there. I don't know why but it wasn't there. So our next plan is going to be bigger."

"Go on, what is it?"

Piper began," Bell is an old cow. She's seen a lot and knows a lot. Unlike Charlie who is too young to sense a trap, she can. The element of surprise must be there!"

"And what trap are we going to use?" they asked.

"I don't know. I will have to think about it" and back to the barn he went.

"How will he think about it in the barn?" asked Charlie to the horse.

"Well, he will start by ramming his pen until an idea hits him, or", the horse stopped.

"Or what", questioned Charlie.

"Or said the horse, something falls off the barn".

"That's what he was doing the first time I talked to him"

"Right", said the horse.

By the time Mack made it to the new spot, Bell was ambling up from the pond to the fence. "Well, what did they say?" demanded Bell, "Do they have something planned for me?"

"Yes, replied Mack

"Come on out with it!" Said an uneasy Bell.

"I don't know yet. Piper said that he had to think about it. There will be no warning this time. It will just happen."

"That's just fine, because you will tell me what it is and then I can look out for it", she nervously thought.

"That's right, said Mack. I will go back over there when Charlie comes out. I hope by then Piper will have an idea. "Then Mack took off to his hole in the barn and Bell went back to the pond.

Chapter 15

The next morning was glorious for that was the day Charlie could go to the barn again. It had been weeks and weeks since he had tangled with the bull.

"Morning", said the chickens as Charlie walked by them.

"Morning", said the pigs.

"Morning", said voices from the milking stall.

"Well don't we look good today", said a voice,

"Yes, I do", said Charlie.

"Aren't you the modest one today", said the voice.

"Yes, Bell, I am, said Charlie.

"Would you like to sit next to me and talk?" asked Bell.

"Yes, I would", remarked Charlie. Looking around at the other cows who were saying under their breaths, "no", but Charlie went down and sat with her anyway.

"How you doing?" questioned Bell.

"Not bad, since I got over that bull business, replied Charlie. How are you?"

Bell thought and said in her most heartfelt voice almost as smooth as butter, "Much better since you are back in the barn". The other cows shot glares at her and murmurs went through the stalls.

"Glad to hear that", said Charlie. With that he got up, stretched, and laid down next to the stall.

Chapter 16

After milking, the cows went to graze and Piper was there also. Charlie sat next to him.

"So did Bell say anything interesting?" asked Piper.

"Not too much", replied Charlie.

"I see," said Piper.

"What and when is our big surprise going to be?"

"Don't know, need to think more," replied Piper. He went back to the barn to think.

As Charlie was coming out of the field he heard two animals talking, one was Bell. But who was she talking to? Charlie stood in the shadow of the barn and listened.

"So what did they say? asked Bell

"Well, said a small voice, Charlie asked what the surprise was and Piper said he had to think about it"

"Good, you did well, Mack here is some corn". Bell gave her small friend the corn she had taken out of her feeder at milking time. As Bell walked off Charlie could see the mouse.

"Well I see we have a spy on our hands. Better inform Piper and fast", Charlie retorted. He ran in haste to Piper's barn. "Piper', yelled Charlie.

"Over here. yelled Piper. What is it?" as he was butting his head.

"Well, I heard Bell talking, Charlie lowered his voice, then replied come with me". Piper looked confused but went with the dog. When they arrived at an area where Charlie thought they were safe, he told Piper what he saw and heard.

"Well then let's adjust our next meeting", said Piper. He whispered what was going to happen. Then he told Charlie to tell the rest and he would hope the spy would be there also.

Chapter 17

That afternoon Charlie sat on the porch until the animals came. When Piper got there the meeting started. "This is another meeting in an attempt to get back at Bell", replied Piper. Addressing the crowd he continued, "Do you have any ideas?"

"Let's soften the bank on the pond where she always goes," shouted the pig.

"We could put rocks in the soft ground so she loses her balance," replied the horse.

"Good ideas" said Piper. "Then pigs you soften the ground, horse you get the rocks, and the cows can put them in place. The chickens can sit at the top of the hill and let us know when she is coming.

"O.K." chorused the animals.

Charlie added, "I will get Bell. She'll need a reason to come to the pond."

"Any questions", asked Piper? The animals appeared to be disturbed about the plan but said nothing. "Good, see you in the morning at the pond", replied Piper. With the plan ready for action the animals made their way back to their place at the farm.

Mack who was on top of the door made his exit unaware that Charlie had seen him up there and watched him leave.

"Do you think he got the message?" asked Piper?

"Yes, I do", replied Charlie still watching Mack run out of sight.

"Let's just hope he got it all", replied Piper. Then Piper and Charlie moseyed down to the barn. Mack went to the fence post where he would meet Bell.

"Well what is the plan?" she asked? Mack told her. "Well that is odd she replied, but I will play along." She gave Mack some grain and they parted ways for the day.

Chapter 18

The next day, when Piper made it to the pond, the pigs were busy at work. "That will work nicely. Now where are the rocks?" asked Piper. Just then the horse came over the hill with a cart of rocks and dumped them where the cows wanted them. The Chickens were policing the area looking for Bell to come to the pond as usual. By the time Charlie arrived the task was done. Piper was smoothing it out with his horns.

"Looks good, remarked Charlie and the farmer is about done milking. So it is about time to get Bell, but I need an idea as to how to get her here. Any ideas?"

The horse said, "I could get in the middle of this and say I need help and she is the only one that can help because of her size and experience". The others looked at him and said,

"Well that would work. She's got you out of a jam before." Charlie looked at the horse. The horse smiled and said, "Long story, I will tell you when you are older. The horse walked into position. Then Charlie ran into the barn, "Bell, he said come quick the horse is stuck in the pond. He told me to get you and that you would know what to do."

"Oh, said Bell not getting too worked up over it, what did he do this time?"

"I do not know but he is stuck. Charlie was trying to act nervous. He then ran out of the barn and back to the pond where the others were waiting for him.

"How did she take it"? asked Piper.

"Not too bad but you could tell that she knew about it", replied Charlie.

"Great, we know that mouse and she had talked", replied Piper. But before he could finish talking to Charlie the chickens were cackling the alarm. "The cows are coming and Bell is leading the herd".

In a big booming voice Bell asked, "What are you doing in there?"

"Well, lied the horse, I was getting a drink and I felt something next to me so I moved. He then stopped and thought for a moment and continued.... when I moved I slipped back and now I am in this sink hole.

"I could get a stick and have you hang on to it but then I would get stuck." replied Bell

"Why would you get stuck?" questioned the horse. "You would be on solid ground".

"I can see that the ground is turned up where I am suppose to stand. I can also see that you are standing on rocks. I would just be in the mud and get stuck. You would all laugh at me and say that this was for a good reason."

The animals looked at each other, and the horse said, "No, we wanted to see your skill in problem solving." This comment appealed to Bell's ego.

"Then get me a very long stick", demanded Bell.

"Thanks, said the horse to Bell.

"No problem. But next time don't make the trick so easy, then Bell with the other cows walked back to the barn.

Chapter 19

"Well, said the horse to Piper, that didn't work so well. She was actually going to pulling me out".

"But it did work well"' said Piper looking off into the distance. Charlie had left the pond and was now cornering something at the third fence post.

"What do you have there?" asked an old voice.

"Oh you know just a mouse". Replied Charlie

"Good. I bet it is our spy is it not?"

"I think it is, Piper", said Charlie. "Let's take him up to the porch where we can really talk to him." Charlie picked up Mack and carried him up the porch, with Mack saying," please Charlie don't eat me, please". When Charlie made it to the porch he was so sick of hearing,

"Don't eat me!" that he contemplated giving him to the cat to play with. But since he had to get information out of him, he had second thoughts. Charlie put him on the porch to have a meeting. "First, to get things moving before all the others show up let's talk. I will not eat you. You will give me heartburn. If I would do anything to you it would be to give you to the farmer's cat". Charlie moved over to his blanket and sat down.

When the others made it to the porch, Mack was horrified to think that he was now on the agenda for the meeting. He was there in the middle of it all instead of listening perched on the door. He was thinking he might make a run for it but the cat was sitting next to the porch as if to say "just try it." Before Mack could make up his mind he heard an old voice talking to him.

"Mouse! What is your name?"

"Mack", quaked the mouse.

"What was your mission for secretly attending our meeting?"

"To stop you from getting Bell into trouble and get some of that grain the farmer feeds the cows at milking time."

"I see, as you know Bell had Charlie go after the bull. We thought that we would get back at her for it", said the old voice.

Mack thought for something to say then he stopped, paused for a moment and looked at them. In his loudest most commanding voice he said, "I thought we were suppose to forgive others and not seek revenge, aren't we?"

The animals stopped and looked at each other then at Mack; "Continue" said the voice.

Mack thought again and then started. "You know, two wrongs do not make a right. At the end the only one you hurt is yourself. Look at this meeting for starters, you are trying to get back at Bell for something most of you would have loved to do because you did not like the dog. So she did it, and then she became the bad one".

With guilt in their eyes, the animals stopped and looked at each other again. They looked at Charlie who looked like he had lost all his friends.

"But there is one animal out of all of you who did like Charlie and that is the same animal who is questioning me right now. He is Charlie's real friend, Piper, not you animals.

You're only here because someone is being questioned about something all of you did.

"Well, said the horse, I never saw it like that",

"Nor did I said the pigs.

"Then I guess we should go and say sorry to Bell, all of us", exclaimed Piper.

"And we should say sorry to Charlie since it was all of you that got him into this mess in the first place" remarked Mack. After a few minutes all of them said that they were sorry and Charlie accepted their apology. Then Charlie leading the pack with Mack on his back set off to the fence post where Bell was waiting for Mack.

Chapter 20

"**H**i", said Charlie to Bell.

"Hello". Said Bell"

Hi too", said the small voice on the back of Charlie.

"What are you doing with them?" snapped Bell.

"I was caught by Charlie".

"I saw him at our last meeting and saw him this morning at this post so I picked him up and took him in for questioning", said Charlie.

"I can't believe you went to the other side," said Bell. She started to walk away but Piper blocked the way." You just stop and listen to what they have to say. Even Charlie has something to say to you". All the animals were telling Bell how wrong they had been for plotting revenge on her.

Charlie came over and sat next to Bell and said, "You know that wasn't nice of you to send me to the bull, nor was it nice of us to try to hurt you. But it was your little friend that found the courage to tell us that. I say this from all of us please accept our apologizes."

Bell stood there and thought and then said, "No, why should I?" She ran past Piper and into the barn.

Chapter 21

"That went over like a lead balloon", said the horse. "She will find out that we are still her friends. If she needs us we will be there," said Mack as, a huge black thunder cloud passed over.

"I see there is a storm coming", said Piper. "I think it is going to be a bad one. Let's all get back into our pens before it hits. Mack where is your hole?"

"Under the barn. Why?"

"I think this storm may fill it. Why don't you stay in my place in the barn", suggested Piper.

"Really, I can?" asked Mack.

"Yes, let's go" replied Piper. They all ran to their area to sit out the storm. What a storm it was. For hours the storm thrashed about with lightning, thunder, and the whole nine yards.

By day break it was over and the animals came out to see what had happened. There was debris all over. Pieces of the barn had fallen off and trees were down.

"What a storm", said Mack to Piper.

"Hope everyone is all right", said Piper. They started to take a head count. Charlie was all ready up and out. He had also been in the barn looking around.

"Well, let's see what's happened out here? It looked like a war zone. All the animals were looking to see if they were all together.

"How are you doing"? asked the pig to the horse.

"Alright, and you"?

"Not Bad!"The chickens were looking for food already. All the animals decided to go to the milking barn. When they got there the cows were in a fuss.

"What's wrong? asked Charlie

"Last night, when the storm hit, Bell was so upset about the meeting that she went out. We asked her not to but she said that we didn't care. After she left we heard a big crash and a concerning *mmoooooo*. It was too bad to go out to see. We have not seen her since. We are worried."

"You did the right thing by not going out in that storm, but we must find her", said Charlie with a bit of worry in his eyes. They all went outside. There under a tree limb alive, but barely, laid Bell.

Chapter 22

"**B**ell", cried Charlie running for her.

"I'll get the farmer," said Piper and took off for the house.

When Charlie reached Bell he could see that her leg was broken and bleeding.

"Bell", cried Charlie again.

"Charlie?" questioned Bell in a very weak voice.

"Yes, it's, me"

"Why did you come to find me?" she asked.

"Because that's what friends are for".

"But I thought…she never finished her sentence, Charlie stopped her because he smelled something in the air.

"Everybody get back. Mack you stay with Bell don't let her stop talking".

"OK, but what should I say to her?"

"Anything, just don't have her fall asleep until the farmer and the vet arrived.

"What's Wrong?" the animals questioned Charlie.

"WOLVES!" As Charlie finished his statement a pack came up to the field heading toward Bell.

Chapter 23

"Run", yelled the chickens

"What about Charlie? I hope Piper and the farmer get here soon. We don't know if Charlie can defend her for long." Said the pig.

"I have an idea" said the horse. He galloped to the other side of the pasture.

As Charlie tried to fend off the attackers, Piper was just getting to the farmer. The wolf pack making it to Charlie stopped.

"What are you doing?" asked the Leader.

"I am doing my job of trying to stop you from hurting my friend", replied Charlie.

"How are you going to do that? There is one of you and five of us", asked the leader.

As Charlie was thinking up a good answer the horse had made it to the Bull's pen at the Harvey's Farm. "Hey", yelled the horse.

"What?"asked the bull. When he came within eye reach he said, "Oh it's you horse.

How is that dog? I hope I didn't kill it. I couldn't believe that Bell would do that to him.

If I had known it was your dog I would just have left it alone. Why are you here anyway? "

"I need a favor from you" and the horse told the Bull about the wolves.

"Lead the way" said the Bull.

Chapter 24

At the other side of the pasture Bell was trapped under the tree, Mack was trying to keep her awake. He had her repeating the ABC's. Bell finally asked Mack, "Why are they doing this for me?"

"We are your friends and friends do not let friends down no matter what"

"That is nice", said Bell, but I think I need to sleep".

"Bell, said Mack. BELL!"

But she had gone to sleep. "No!" said Mack I hope the farmer and Piper get here soon"

Meanwhile Charlie was still trying to figure out how he was going to stop the wolves.

"Well, how are you going to stop us?"

"With help", bellowed a voice. As Charlie and the wolves looked over the hill the horse and the bull running side by side bulldozed the wolves. The wolves tumbled down the hill. Behind the bulldoze team came the farmer yelling and shooting. The wolves scrambled to their feet and made a fast retreat over the fence. "Next time dog, next time", they yipped.

The bull yelled back, "His name is Charlie. He's one of the best dogs I know".

The horse said to the Bull "They're gone Bull. Maybe you should say what you want to say to Charlie before his ego grows."

"Alright, but first let's help Bell".

Chapter 25

When the farmer made it to Bell, the Bull and the horse had managed to get the tree off of Bell.

"Bell, oh Bell, said the farmer I must get you to a vet," as he called on his cell phone.

"Well", said the Bull to Charlie, who was a bit surprised to see him, I need to tell you something".

"What is that?" asked Charlie way looking for a good place to run.

"I didn't know you were their dog. I have scared other dogs before. Bell and the old dog were good friends so I believe that is why she had you come over. I didn't have my contacts in therefore I didn't know who you were. I am very sorry. Could you find a place in your heart to forgive me?"

Charlie thought for a moment, and said, "You did almost kill me".

"I know. I'm, very sorry, however, you did with the help of the horse save Bell, Mack the mouses life and me so I can forgive you." Said Charlie.

"Thank you and if you would like to talk, all you have to do is just go to that fence over there, pointing with his left hoof, and we can talk. He then went back to his farm.

Chapter 26

The vet arrived and started to check over Bell, The animals backed away and let him work. By the next morning, Bell was not in the meadow but in a closed stable for almost a month. Then on day the vet arrived and let her out.

"She's as good as I could make her. You will have her milking in no time. Just try to keep her indoors during big storms", remarked the vet. With that the farmer paid the vet and the animals came to see Bell.

"How are you? asked the cows?"

"I am fine answered Bell, dramatically. Where is Mack?"

"I'm down here!"

Bell looked down and saw him on the floor. He ran up the post, onto her big nose and hugged it.

"Thank you", she said and thanks all of you who tried to save me even if you didn't have to".

"You are welcome", they chorused.

"Now, if you don't mind, I would like to rest "said Bell.

As they were leaving, Charlie and Piper walked in. "How are you doing?" they asked.

"Not bad" How are you two? "I am sorry I was so very mean to you. I know you didn't have to save me. You could have just walked away, but you didn't. That made me think of what I tried to do to Charlie".

"Yes," he said

"Can you forgive me the same way you did the bull?"

Charlie said, "Bell, I forgave you before I saved you".

"We all did".

"Why don't we let you rest?"

"Sounds good!"

The three of them, Charlie, Piper and Mack walked out of the barn.

"Hey Piper", called Mack, Can I sleep in you pen again tonight"

"I guess you can" They all laughed.

Printed in the USA
CPSIA information can be obtained
at www.ICGtesting.com
CBHW061303111024
15667CB00033B/234